To Christina

Believe!

Love, Carmel

Copyright © 2015 Carmel Rivello
Artwork by Toby Mikle of MyBookIllustrator.com
All rights reserved.
ISBN: : 978-0-9967551-0-8

DEDICATION

To all the children of the world who are lonely and find new friends and to my daughters, Michel, Regina, Derryn and Angela and to my grandchildren, Christopher, Sara Rose and Greyson Paul who are my friends, and who give me constant joy

ACKNOWLEDGMENTS

To Gerald Barney, who provides me daily with ideas and concepts to fulfill my dreams

Bella was a tan bunny with large bright eyes, pink floppy ears and a smile like sunshine on a dewdrop. She lived in the back of farmer Sam's garden, under a large white Angel trumpet tree, and Bella had everything she needed for a wonderful life. She even had a tiny garden of her own, where she grew delicious lettuce, carrots and bright red radishes -- her favorite foods.

Farmer Sam's wife, Lucy, also fed her all kinds of delicious greens from the back door. Oh how she loved the carrots! She loved to nibble on the crusty bread from Lucy's kitchen that she held between her strong rabbit paws.

Bella so loved her little house, her garden and her delicious food, BUT...there was one thing missing...One very big thing -- She was lonely! All her friends had moved away to other gardens and fields, and her own family lived far from Farmer Sam's garden. Her parents had moved into a retirement village, where they played golf and enjoyed other rabbit sports, and watched funny animal movies. All the other boy and girl rabbits had grown up and were now raising families of their own.

Nibble and Hoppy just had their 29th little baby! Oh, how Bella wished she could see them again, and run and play and enjoy bunny treats in her yard. Bella sighed -- her little heart was sad.

There were no playdates, no swings to swing on, no costumes to play dress-up, no bunny toys to share. What should she do? Where should she go? She was so puzzled!

Farmer Sam and his wife Lucy were so kind to her and made her feel right at home. They found her one day in their herb garden, nibbling parsley and basil, and cared for her as if she was one of their own. So why should she feel so sad?

Bella scampered around the edge of the garden, exploring all the posts and fences, and looking out through the wire, hoping to see someone she could talk to, in bunny language, of course! But today, there was no one around.

They had all gone to the fair and bunny farmer's market to buy fruits and vegetables for their families and friends. Delicious foods for everyone! Ohhh, they sold a lot of carrots!

A big tear started to form in Bella's beautiful eyes. "Sniff, sniff," she muffled. It was late afternoon, and she was tired, so she hopped back onto her little bed, and fell asleep.

Soon, Bella started to dream. Beautiful fluffy clouds and twinkling stars and bright rainbows were sprinkled all across the sky.

In her dream Bella was running with all her old friends. They were playing bunny ball, catching fireflies, chasing butterflies and laughing and swinging on the little swing that Farmer Sam had put up on the old apple tree, so long ago.

When it started to rain, Bella woke up and the dream fairies flew away, leaving Bella, once more, lonely and sad.

"I wish my dream were true," Bella sighed. Back out in the yard, a magical sight appeared. She looked up and saw the most caring, magnificent butterfly, with lovely sparkling eyes and a golden color that was so bright, it took Bella's breath away!

"Who…who…what are you?" she asked the beautiful flying creature. Bella was so excited she forgot her manners.

When she finally spoke, Bella told the butterfly, "My name is Bella and I have never seen anything quite as beautiful as you!"

The beautiful Flying creature spoke softly to Bella.

"My name is Flutter, and I am called a butterfly. I can fly high and low and just about everywhere I want to fly, and I can see all over the farms and yards and I drink from delicious flowers…this is my life, and much , much more!

Slowly, very s-l-o-w-l-y, and not to frighten her, Flutter emerged as a little soft person, smiling and with no effort at all, floating around the yard.

Bella was amazed and not at all frightened -- She knew that she was safe, and that Flutter was her friend!

"Now, I see you as another form…where did you come from? Why are you here?"

Flutter smiled with a knowing smile.

"I have come from another place, very far from here -- somewhere you probably have never heard of, and never dreamed of in your little bunny life. I have come to bring you safe and happy feelings, and news of an amazing future for all the people on your beautiful earth.

My world is so very different from yours, and my family and friends and I want to bring you love and joy and friendship. We travel very quickly, from a long distance, from stars and planets far away, to visit you and your world, and we have been doing this for many, many years! Your earth people do not yet know how to do this kind of travel, but they will soon, when our cultures teach them how."

"How…how do you do this", asked Bella? Flutter smiled, a very peaceful and warm, knowing smile.

"Well, it is quite a long story. Do you want to hear about us?"

"Yes, oh yes! -- of course," said Bella, and she settled down on her little bunny bench and the amazing and wondrous story began...

"A very, very long time ago, we were here to help, teach and love you all. What did we do? We left behind many stone forms and buildings -- so many, in fact, that they are still all over your beautiful planet earth. We traveled here because we needed to show you how we do things with our energy. We left many mysterious things that your people are still trying to understand…And that's why I am here today, Bella.

You see, even a little bunny can understand what I am about to tell you. When we come down on our shiny starships, we come with love. Some people just don't believe us and they are sometimes scared. But that is not what we want for you. We bring special signs so that you may understand who we are and why we come to you…

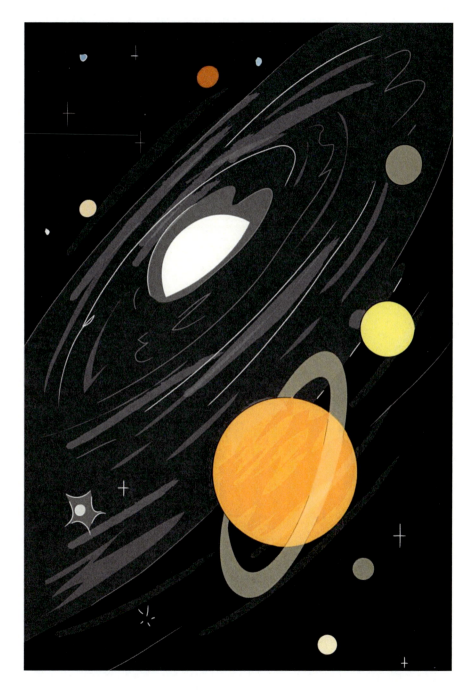

Did you ever see a bright star that seems to be moving very quickly across the sky, then suddenly stop, turn around, and quickly leave the heavens?

That's US!! We are trying to bring you a message of hope and joy. But again, many people try to make us disappear and pretend that it was not really us, but just a make-believe cloud or a big weather balloon.

Bella, it is really us! We have been trying to contact you on earth for many, many years, and finally, we know that your earth people are starting to believe in us, many of them see us and truly want to make contact with us! "We are finally connecting with each other! I am so happy you believe in me!

I am so very happy that you, on your beautiful blue planet are starting to open your arms and hearts, and are asking us to come to earth and visit you! Truly, this

will be a great change for your world!

Bella was so thrilled! Her little ears stood straight up. Her eyes brightened with joy!

Flutter looked at Bella and returned a big, happy smile.

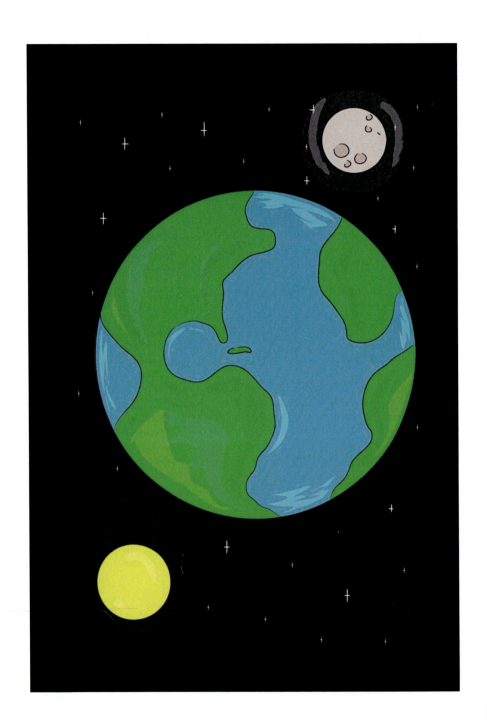

...Then Bella sighed..."But I am so lonely. I have no one to play with and I never see any other bunnies or little friends ....I am really, really sad".

"Your home is quite beautiful", Flutter told Bella, "and it looks like your garden gives you such delicious things to eat."

"Yes, the lady that lives here, Lucy, brings me all sorts of delicious food that I like to nibble on while I sit in the sun.

She and farmer Sam have so much to do…work, computers, iPads, cooking, friends, marketing, cell phones, Yoga classes."

…Then Bella sighed, "But I am so lonely. I have no one to play with and I never see other bunnies or little friends…I am really, really, sad."

"Hmm", said the beautiful butterfly…

"That is indeed a sad thought…no one to play with, no one to laugh with, to have fun with, no one to jump bunny rope with, and no one to share carrots with....hmm. I must go now," and Flutter changed back into a mysterious butterfly, and off she flew, gentle as the breeze and oh so lovely, her wings shimmering in the brilliant sunlight.

Bella shed a soft tear and went under the Angel trumpet tree, onto her bed and because of the exciting day, fell fast asleep.

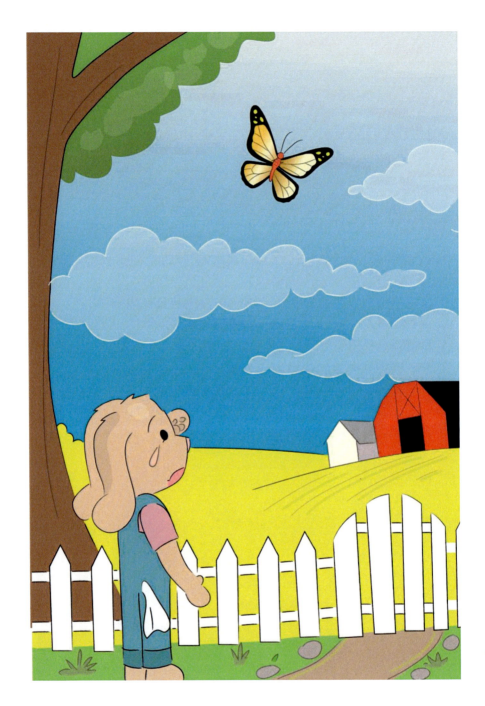

The next morning, as Bella was eating her breakfast, she thought she heard an unusual sound overhead, as though there was a movement in the air. Slowly, she looked up.

She hopped to the clearing in the garden, and stopped quickly, her little bunny ears stood straight up!

Then, there was a great silence and what Bella saw next was breathtaking and brilliant!

A beautiful, shiny silver ship hovered over the land! Out of the ship came many precious little brings, smiling and with love in their eyes and hearts.

The sky was full of the most beautiful flying birds, bees, ladybugs, butterflies, seagulls, eagles, hummingbirds, robins, finches, bright yellow canaries, butterflies, parrots, fairies and elves, leprechauns and little folk... all so rich with many magnificent colors! Winged creatures of every kind...The sky was full of many flying gifts. And at the very front of this magical parade, was ... Flutter!

"I have come to bring you friends, Bella. They all love you and want you never to be lonely again! They want to play with you and share your yard and toys and laughter. The butterflies enrich the flowers, drinking the nectar.

The eagles soar above the earth, creating beauty for everyone to see. The bees drink from flowers and make delicious honey, the hummingbirds collect nectar from each flower …the ladybugs are so good for the plants and flowers. The parrots sing their song and the canaries brighten your day. The little folk bring laughter and the fairies capture your hearts. Every one of your new friends enrich your planet and fill it with happiness. They are the peaceful creatures, bringing you love."

Bella giggled and looked up at Flutter, and gave her a big smile.

Flutter would be her BEST friend forever!

Bella asked Flutter, "How can I see you again?"

Flutter smiled. "Just close your eyes, and think of me, and I will be there!

Now Bella, I have a surprise for you. Do you want to travel with me? I want to show you the universe! I want to show you many different places that you do not know about. I can travel very fast and take you to other civilizations that you and your planet have not yet heard about.

We can travel through space and time in the blink of a bunny's eye. There are many civilizations, and we will travel to there.

These interplanetary relatives are waiting for us, for you and me, to visit.

You see, Bella, we are all ONE, in harmony with each other. Many galaxies are waiting to bring you pure light, peace and hope. They want to contact you on your beautiful blue planet. Our visit can make this happen. There will be a wondrous future ahead for all".

So many new wonders awaited Bella. Her world was expanding and Flutter would be such a teacher, bringing her to new worlds, meeting so many new life forms and hopefully, Flutter's family.

"I will have to pack some bunny clothes", said Bella.

"No need to pack anything. We will just imagine it, and away we will go!"

Bella was so happy! She finally had playmates and was never lonely again!

And her star friend Flutter was the best!

The journey of Bella and Flutter has just begun. There are many wondrous trips ahead... planned by the amazing Flutter and breathlessly awaited by our beautiful friend Bella, the bunny.

And Farmer Sam and his wife Lucy were very happy for Bella! Everyone believed in Bella's new friends, especially the tan bunny with large eyes, pink ears and a smile like sunshine on a dew drop, by the name of Bella.

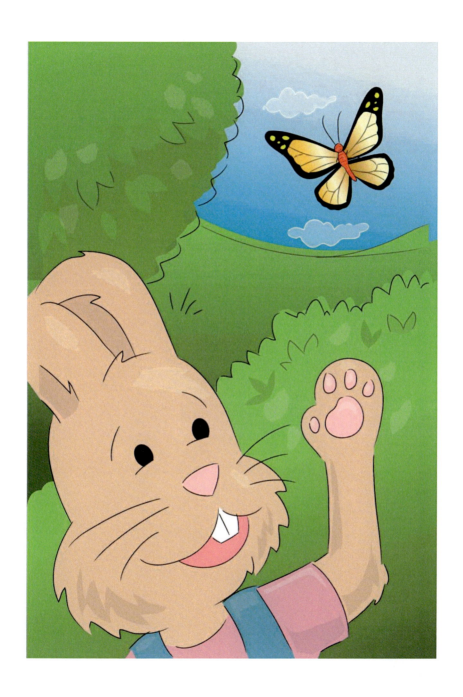

The end – for now

ABOUT THE AUTHOR

Carmel Rivello is the mother of four daughters – two of them published authors – and three grandchildren.

Her love of children, writing and animals prompted her to write *The Bunny and the Mysterious Butterfly*.

Having herself experienced contact with other cosmic beings (who were very kind and benign) made Carmel realize how much-needed it was for children to be introduced to this subject in a gentle loving way. Too many TV productions have created an image of terror.

Extraterrestrial contact need not and should not be a fearful event for children, and by presenting it in a most careful, loving, and enlightening way she strove to teach children about a wondrous world. With the growing "disclosure" movement, the cap of government secrecy about these phenomena has been recently partially removed, thanks to the world of social media and the internet. There are thousands of sightings a year, and those who are prepared can themselves experience contact.

Ms. Rivello is a graduate of California Lutheran University. In addition to writing, she is also a voice-over artist. She lives in Thousand Oaks and Ojai, California.

Made in the USA
San Bernardino, CA
03 November 2015